David's Tractor

By Jami Spinelli

Illustrated By Lois Margolis

David's Tractor
is written by Jami Spinelli
and illustrated by Lois Margolis
Copyright 2006 Jami Spinelli

Published and Printed by:
  Lifevest Publishing
  4901 E. Dry Creek Rd., #170
  Centennial, CO 80122
  www.lifevestpublishing.com

Printed in the United States of America

I.S.B.N. 1-59879-242-3

For my son David and my husband Andy
And to Andy's wonderful parents Guy and Elaine
With All my Love

Daddy got David up early one Saturday morning.
"Where are we going Daddy?" asked David.

"It's a surprise." said Daddy.

They got into Daddy's red truck and started to drive.

David asked, "If they were there yet." His Daddy said, "Not yet, just a little further."

The road started to curve and became very bumpy. Then the red truck turned onto a road and stopped. On the side of the road was a big tractor junkyard. There were tractors of all colors and sizes.

David started to giggle with glee. He loved tractors.

"Is this my surprise Daddy?" David asked.

"Yes it is. We are going to pick out your very own tractor to fix up." said Daddy.

They got out of the truck and started walking around.

How about this red tractor, David?

No it's too new.

Look at this blue one.

No, I do not like blue tractors.

There in the corner stuck in the mud, was a green tractor.

"That's the one, Daddy!" yelled David.

Well let's see if the motor will turn on." said Daddy.

David's Daddy turned the engine on. The engine sputtered, but then conked out.

"Oh no, Daddy, the engine is broken."

"Wait just a moment David. And his Daddy turned the engine on again. All of a sudden the engine burst to life. David started cheering.

"Let's go find the owner of the junkyard." said his Daddy.

They started walking to the house.

An old man walked out and asked if they had found what they were looking for.

David and his Daddy said yes.

They walked with the old man back to the green tractor.

The old man said, "It will take a little while to push it out of the mud, but it's a good find.

David's Daddy and the old man started pushing the tractor. It wouldn't budge. So they got some boards and turned the tractor on and pushed it up onto the boards. David and his Daddy rode the tractor back to the red truck. David got off the tractor so his Daddy could drive it up the ramps into the truck and tie it down. David's Daddy paid the old man and they were on their way home.

When they arrived home, David ran out of the truck to his Mommy.

"Mommy, Mommy, look what I got."

His Mommy said it looked like a great find and that he and Daddy would have fun restoring it.

The green tractor was put into the barn until tomorrow, when they would work on it together. David could hardly wait.

David awoke the next morning, bright and early and ran into his parent's room.

"Is it time yet?"

His Daddy rolled over and said,"Wait just a minute, I have to get ready."

David waited while his Daddy got ready. Together they went out to the barn.

In the barn there were lots of green, red and some orange tractors. They pulled out David's tractor to work on it.

Daddy brought out some spark plugs. He told David that the engine needed new ones to start up better. David helped his Daddy put in the new spark plugs. They turned the engine on. It started right up. David jumped for joy.

His Daddy went back into the barn and came out with some sandpaper to take off the old paint.

After sanding for some time, they took a break for sandwiches and lemonade. After lunch they continued to work on David's tractor.

They worked all day on the tractor. The sun started going down and David wanted to continue. Daddy said he would have to wait until tomorrow. They pulled the tractor back into the barn and went in for dinner.

David talked all evening about the tractor. At bedtime he wanted to see how his tractor was. Mommy told him he would have to wait to see it in the morning. Daddy and Mommy kissed David good night.

The next morning David and his Daddy went to work on the tractor. His Daddy brought out some green paint. David was very excited, the tractor was almost finished.

It took them a couple of days to paint the green tractor, but it was finally finished. It looked perfect. They named it David Jr. David and his Daddy climbed onto the tractor and went for a long ride.

That evening they put the tractor away to rest. They went inside and David thanked his Daddy. And his Daddy said "you're welcome."

He then told David he could show his tractor next year at the Sycamore Tractor Show.

The End

About the Illustrator

Lois Margolis is a retired Executive who lives in Huntley (Sun City) Illinois. After retirement she renewed her love for painting and drawing. This is her first attempt at illustrating a children's book. She found it challenging and exciting.

About the Author

Jami Spinelli is a stay at home mom. She lives with her husband and son in Woodstock, Illinois. She was inspired to write this book because of her husband Andy and their son David's love of tractors. She has always enjoyed writing children's stories, but this is her first book to be published. She hopes to have many more books in the series to be published.

David's Tractor

by **Jami Spinelli**
Illustrations by Lois Margolis

I.S.B.N. 1-59879-242-3

Order Online at:
www.authorstobelievein.com

By Phone Toll Free at:
1-877-843-1007